GHOST DETECTORS

I'm Gonna Get You!

BOOK 2

BY
DOTTI ENDERLE

ILLUSTRATED BY
HOWARD MCWILLIAM

magic
wagon

visit us at www.abdopublishing.com

A special thanks to Melissa Markham — DE
For Grandad Bill — HM

Text by Dotti Enderle
Illustrations by Howard McWilliam
Edited by Stephanie Hedlund and Rochelle Baltzer
Cover and interior design by Jaime Martens

Library of Congress Cataloging-in-Publication Data

Enderle, Dotti, 1954-
   I'm gonna get you! / by Dotti Enderle ; illustrated by Howard
McWilliam.
      p. cm. -- (Ghost Detectors ; bk. 2)
   Summary: While his great-grandmother seeks her deceased
husband, ten-year-old Malcolm and his best friend Dandy have
no trouble finding a ghost on which to test Malcolm's latest
gadget--a ghost zapper.
   ISBN 978-1-60270-691-0
   [1. Ghosts--Fiction. 2. Haunted houses--Fiction. 3. Great-
grandmothers--Fiction. 4. Family life--Fiction. 5. Humorous
stories.] I. McWilliam, Howard, 1977- ill. II. Title. III. Title: I
am gonna get you! IV. Title: I am going to get you!
   PZ7.E69645Iam 2009
   [Fic]--dc22
                                        2008055331

Contents

Wait . . . Wait . . . Wait

Malcolm waited on his front porch steps. He craned his neck to the right, looking as far down the street as possible.

His best friend, Dandy, sat next to him. Dandy wiggled his finger in his ear like he was trying to loosen something.

"Where is she?" Malcolm said.

"What?" Dandy asked.

"I've been waiting for weeks, and today is finally the day. I can't believe she's late." Malcolm got up and started to pace in front of the porch.

"What?" Dandy repeated.

Malcolm sighed and then removed Dandy's finger from his ear. "She's never this late."

Dandy shrugged. "Oh. Well, maybe she had an emergency."

Malcolm thought about that. "What kind of emergency would a mail carrier have?"

"Maybe she had to deliver a baby." Dandy put his finger back into his ear and jiggled it some more.

"She's a mail carrier, Dandy, not a stork!"

Malcolm sat back down and tapped his foot impatiently. He had already used his

Ecto-Handheld-Automatic-Heat-Sensitive-Laser-Enhanced Specter Detector. It worked well. Too well!

Malcolm cringed. He still had nightmares about the major wedgie that prankster ghost, Herbert McBleaky, had given him.

After that experience, Malcolm had decided that it was no use detecting a ghost if you couldn't get rid of it. So Malcolm had ordered an Ecto-Handheld-Automatic-Heat-Sensitive-Laser-Enhanced Ghost Zapper. And he intended to use it!

Dandy looked at his fingers, then burrowed into his other ear. "You never told me the plan. Are we going after Herbert McBleaky?"

"Naw. I think we should detect a tamer ghost first and use the zapper on him."

"But where are we going to find a tamer ghost?"

"There are ghosts everywhere," Malcolm told him. "We'll just go on a ghost hunt."

Dandy's face brightened. "Yeah! Like a treasure hunt!" Then he paused. "Except we'd find something scary instead of something fun."

"No one said ghost detecting would be fun," Malcolm said. "It's certainly not for the weak of heart." Although as Malcolm said it, he wasn't so sure he was really all that brave.

Dandy gave him a blank stare. It was the same look he gave his mom when she'd ask if he'd cleaned his room. "If it isn't fun, then why are we even doing it?"

Didn't Dandy understand anything? "For the greater good," Malcolm replied. "We'll rid the world of all the stray ghosts. I mean, think about it. They're just hanging out, making houses uninhabitable."

Dandy gave him that blank look again.

"*Uninhabitable* means no one can live there," Malcolm informed him.

"Oh," Dandy said, still drilling into his ear.

Malcolm squinted his eyes, looking down the street for Mail Carrier Nancy. He began to wonder if she really did have an emergency.

Or maybe she called in sick, and her replacement used a different route. He tapped his foot some more. He was close to jumping up and running down the street to look for her.

Just when he thought he might actually fly out of his own skin, he saw her turn the corner. She was pulling her mail cart and zigzagging from house to house.

Dandy took his finger out of his ear, smelled it, then wiped it on his Iron Man T-shirt. Malcolm and Dandy both stood as Mail Carrier Nancy approached, a smile beaming from her face.

"I have a package for you," she told Malcolm.

"Yes!" he cheered, meeting her halfway. She dug into the cart. Still wearing a smile, she came up with the package and a few other letters for Malcolm's family.

Her look quickly changed as she glanced behind Malcolm. She now shuddered in terror. Her eyes grew large and her mouth formed a perfect O.

Malcolm knew of only one creature that could put that look of horror on a person's face. He had a feeling that what stood behind him was the most terrifying thing on Earth.

Blackmail

A hand clamped down on Malcolm's shoulder and he quickly spun around. His sister, Cocoa, stood there sneering. It was exactly as he'd feared.

"What'd you do with it?" she barked. She wore electric blue eye shadow and lip gloss so orange it reminded Malcolm of a hazard sign. Some had smeared onto her front teeth. She dug her plum purple fingernails into Malcolm's collarbone.

Malcolm grew pale. "Go away."

"Not until you tell me what you did with it!" Cocoa leaned so close he could smell the tuna fish sandwich still lingering on her breath.

"Just tell her," Dandy begged. He slowly backed away, like he might scream and sprint off at any moment.

"I don't even know what she's talking about," Malcolm said.

Cocoa squinted at him. "I'm talking about my iPod, loser. I know you took it."

True, Malcolm had snuck her iPod out of her room. He'd heard of people picking up spirit messages on walkie-talkies and in TV static. Ghosts liked communicating through electronics. He figured if Cocoa could download music on it, then maybe he could rig it to download ghost voices.

So, he'd simply converted her iPod into an apparition-receiving device. Once it was

perfected, he'd planned to call it *iHaunts – Voices from Beyond.*

"Give it back, dweeb!" Cocoa demanded.

"Uh-hum." Mail Carrier Nancy cleared her throat. "Here's your mail."

Malcolm reached for it, but Cocoa was quicker. She snatched it away so fast, Malcolm felt like he was in a time warp.

"Hey!" he cried as Cocoa headed back up the sidewalk. "That's my package!"

"Yeah? You can have it when I get my iPod back!" She gave him a sneer that could only be seen in a carnival spook house. Even Mail Carrier Nancy cringed.

"Do something," Malcolm told Dandy.

Dandy stuck his finger back in his ear. "She's your sister."

Mail Carrier Nancy clutched her cart. "Good luck, boys." She hurried away.

"I want my package!" Malcolm yelled as he stormed into the house. Dandy followed, doing a double step to catch up.

"You know the deal," Cocoa said, slamming and locking her bedroom door.

Malcolm wasn't going to take this. He'd dealt with Cocoa way too many times to let this one slide. He'd been waiting more than six weeks for that package! So he did the one thing he knew he had to do. "MOM!"

Malcolm stomped into the kitchen where his mother sat, making a grocery list. Just as he started to protest, she looked up, relief in her eyes.

"Malcolm, would you please get your toy away from Grandma Eunice? She's driving me crazy."

Grandma Eunice was actually Malcolm's great-grandmother. She'd been living with them as long as he could remember.

Just as his mother spoke, Grandma Eunice came creaking into the kitchen in her wheelchair. She held the Ecto-Handheld-Automatic-Heat-Sensitive-Laser-Enhanced Specter Detector in her hand. She was swinging it back and forth, aiming it at nothing.

"Where are you, you son of a gun?" she called. She gazed intensely at the air in the room.

"Who are you looking for?" Malcolm asked.

"Who do you think?" she said. "Your great-grandpa Bertram."

"Grandma Eunice," Mom sighed. "Grandpa Bertram died in 1977."

"But he's still haunting me. He used to bring me jellybeans!" She swung around, aiming the ghost detector into the dining room. "Bertram! I want more jellybeans!"

"Malcolm," Mom said, trying to stay patient, "please take your toy back to the basement."

Malcolm gestured for Grandma Eunice to give it up. "Hand it over, Grandma. You're not even using it right."

She gave it to Dandy instead. "Here, Alfred," she whined. "No one around here plays fair."

Malcolm knew that Mom wasn't up for another crisis. He'd have to deal with Cocoa himself.

"Come on, Dandy." The boys headed for Cocoa's bedroom.

"Dude," Dandy said, "your family is bonkers."

Malcolm looked at Dandy, who had one finger in his ear and the other up his nose.

"Yeah," he agreed. Down the hall he could hear Grandma Eunice shout, "Bertram, I want my jellybeans!"

Superweapon

Malcolm handed Cocoa her iPod, and she slapped the package into his chest.

"Now go away!" she screamed, slamming the door. Malcolm was more than happy to leave.

He and Dandy hurried down to his lab in the basement. His heart was pumping faster again. The excitement had returned.

"Do you have any idea how high tech this is?" Malcolm asked Dandy as he ripped the tape off the box.

Dandy didn't answer. He just stood rubbing his belly, waiting to see what was inside.

Even though the box was big, Malcolm could see that it was mostly filled with Bubble Wrap. He began unwrapping it. The unwinding seemed to take forever. Finally, he had it in his hand. His very own Ecto-Handheld-Automatic-Heat-Sensitive-Laser-Enhanced Ghost Zapper.

"Uh . . . that's it?" Dandy asked. They both stared at the object Malcolm held.

Dandy scratched his nose. "Shouldn't it be bigger?"

Malcolm wondered the same thing. The ad in the back of *Worlds Beyond* magazine made it look like a megamachine. But it looked more like an aerosol can with a trigger. Even the laser was hidden.

"It looks like my mom's hairspray," Dandy added.

Malcolm reached back into the box and pulled out the instructions. He read them out loud.

Your Ecto-Handheld-Automatic-Heat-Sensitive-Laser-Enhanced Ghost Zapper is the perfect companion to the Ecto-Handheld-Automatic-Heat-Sensitive-Laser-Enhanced Specter Detector. Once a ghost has been detected, shake well, aim, and squeeze the trigger.

CAUTION: USE ONLY AS DIRECTED.

"That seems easy enough," Dandy said. "Are we going on a ghost hunt now?"

Malcolm shrugged. He was truly disappointed. All this time he'd pictured himself lugging a superweapon that would disintegrate any ghost in his path. This thing looked more like something he'd use

to spray graffiti on them. But still, it must work. There was only one way to find out.

"Yeah," Malcolm said, "I think we might need to search out a ghost . . . you know . . . to test it."

Dandy's face split into a huge grin, but then he tried to look serious. "Where do we start?"

"I think we should just keep the ghost detector on all the time," Malcolm said. "Let the ghosts find us."

"Like your great-grandpa?" Dandy asked with a straight face.

"What? No!" Malcolm said. "Grandma Eunice is just being silly."

"But you never know. After all, I was there too. I know she isn't batty," Dandy whispered, looking around the room.

Malcolm switched the ghost detector to On. Once it warmed up, he flipped it to Detect. They both looked around, waiting.

Finally Malcolm said, "See? No Grandpa Bertram. Besides, I think I could sense if my own house was haunted."

That's when the basement door flew open with a bang. Cocoa came stomping down the stairs. "Hey creep, aren't you forgetting something?"

Malcolm rolled his eyes. "Yeah, I forgot to lock the door!"

"You forgot about dogsitting!"

Yikes! Malcolm had been worrying so much about his package arriving that he'd forgotten he'd promised to feed the Millers' dogs while they were on vacation. And they'd left last night.

"Can't you do it?" Malcolm asked Cocoa.

"And have a sneezing fit? You know I'm allergic to dogs."

Malcolm remembered Cocoa's last sneezing fit. Her nose turned purple and her pea green eye shadow ran down to her cheeks, mixing with her maroon blush. She'd looked like a clown on meltdown. Yuck!

"Fine," Malcolm said. "I'm going." He tucked his ghost detector into the waistband of his jeans. Then he and Dandy headed out.

Dogsitting

Malcolm squinted against the afternoon sun as he and Dandy headed down the sidewalk. He couldn't believe he'd forgotten to feed the dogs.

Dandy was humming. Malcolm had no idea what tune it was though. It sounded like a cross between "Pop Goes the Weasel" and the theme from *Star Trek*.

"So we're just going to dump some food in their bowls then go ghost hunting, right?" Dandy asked.

"It's not just feeding them," Malcolm said. "It's dogsitting. I have to pet them and play with them. You know, make sure they're not lonely."

Dandy looked at him like it was the first day of school. "How long will that take?"

Malcolm sighed. "I don't know. Until the dogs are tired of us, I guess."

"And you have to do this for how long?"

"Just for a week."

Dogsitting wasn't new to Malcolm. He'd taken care of the Millers' dogs last summer too. And they had really cool dogs. Both were bassett hounds. One named Brom, the other named Bowser.

The boys crossed the street and walked around to the Millers' backyard. Malcolm

dug a key out from under a rock in the flowerbed, then unlocked the gate. Bowser and Brom were already there waiting. Their barks were like the last dying putts of a lawn mower.

"Hey, fellas!" Malcolm said, rubbing their necks. "Hungry?"

Brom padded over and nudged Dandy. Dandy reached down to pet him. "Wow, he's so . . . saggy."

Brom bellowed cheerfully, then rolled over for a belly rub.

"Look. He's just like you," Malcolm said with a grin.

Malcolm found the dog food sealed in a plastic tub on the back porch. Both dogs rushed him—as much as a bassett hound can rush. He scooped out a huge bowlful for each. Dandy petted Bowser as he ate.

Next Malcolm turned on the hose and cleaned out their water trough. He filled it up again and turned to Dandy. "Now the fun part."

"We play ball with them?" Dandy asked.

"Not yet." Malcolm grabbed a shovel and a bucket. "First, poop patrol."

"What?" Dandy rubbed his own belly the same way he'd rubbed Brom's earlier.

"Poop patrol," Malcolm repeated. "We can't leave it scattered all over the yard."

"Sure, we can," Dandy argued.

Malcolm gave him a look. "Come on. I've nearly stepped in it twice already." Malcolm handed Dandy the bucket. He kept the shovel. "I'll scoop."

Every time Malcolm dumped his find into the bucket, Dandy said, "Bleck!"

Once the last poop was scooped, Dandy picked up the ball. "Now do we play?"

"Go ahead," Malcolm told him. "I need to make sure their doghouse is clean."

The Millers' doghouse looked more like a playhouse than a place for dogs to sleep. Malcolm ducked in to straighten their doggie beds, but quickly jumped back. A small white dog cowered in the corner, shivering.

"Hey, little fellow," Malcolm said softly. "Where did you come from?" He hadn't realized that the Millers had gotten a new dog. He still only saw two beds. And the only bowls said *Brom* and *Bowser.*

Hmmm . . . Maybe the Millers got this dog right before they left.

"It's okay," Malcolm assured the little dog. "I'm not going to hurt you." But

when he reached closer, it whimpered and thumped his tail. "All right, all right."

Malcolm backed out and grabbed more dog food. "The Millers have a new dog," he told Dandy.

Dandy stopped in mid-pitch, holding the slobbery ball he'd been tossing to the bassett hounds. "Where?"

"It's hiding in the doghouse."

Malcolm peeked in again. The dog stayed curled in the corner. "Here you go," he said, putting a small pile of food on the floor.

Malcolm waited. The dog just sat, shaking. He was afraid if he touched it the dog might snap. Better to leave it alone.

He went over to Dandy, who was wrestling the ball away from Brom. "Are they exhausted yet?" Malcolm asked.

"I don't think so." Dandy was panting harder than the dogs.

Malcolm snatched the ball from Brom's teeth, then jogged to the other side of the yard for a good throwing distance. That's when something in the kitchen window caught his eye. Just a glimpse, but it was real.

"Did you see that?" he asked Dandy.

"What?"

Malcolm crept over and peeked in. No lights were on. The house was covered in afternoon shadows. But Malcolm saw a man near the refrigerator.

Someone was inside the Millers' house!

9-1-1!

Malcolm ducked. Was he imagining things?

"Dandy," he whispered. He motioned for Dandy to come over.

"What'ya hiding from?" Dandy asked in a voice loud enough to scare off birds. Brom and Bowser were jumping at him, trying to get the ball.

"Shhhh!" Malcolm put a finger to his lips.

Dandy's face went blank for a moment.

Then he tiptoed over. He squatted by Malcolm under the window. Bowser and Brom followed.

"Someone's inside the Millers' house." Malcolm tried to remain calm, but his heart was thumping against his chest at record speed.

Dandy paused a moment, taking it all in. Then he asked, "Is it a man or a woman?"

"A man."

"Short or tall?"

"Tall . . . I think."

"Thin or fat?"

"Thin," Malcolm said.

"Blond hair or brown?"

"I don't know," Malcolm whispered.

"Did he have a huge, hairy mole by his nose?"

"What? I don't know, I don't think so. What difference does it make?"

Dandy leaned in. "Because if he's tall, thin, and blonde with a hairy mole, it could be Darren Von Datton, the famous diamond smuggler."

Malcolm just stared. "Do you really think the Millers have valuable diamonds hidden in their house?"

"You never know."

"I know," Malcolm said. "They don't, otherwise they would hire someone to watch their dogs instead of having the neighbor kid do it!"

Dandy rolled the ball away so Bowser and Brom would stop jumping at him. "So what now?"

"I have to be sure," Malcolm said. Inch by inch, he slowly raised himself up. He took a deep breath. Then Malcolm dared another peek. The man was still there, hovering by the fridge. Malcolm dropped back down by Dandy. "He's still there."

"Maybe it's Mr. Miller," Dandy suggested. "He could've come home early."

"But the dogs hadn't been fed. Mr. Miller would have fed them. Besides, it doesn't look like Mr. Miller."

"Maybe it's a relative. You know, an uncle or something?"

Malcolm shook his head. "The house is dark inside. Someone staying here would turn on a lamp or something."

Bowser and Brom were back, nudging Dandy. The rubber ball, full of teeth marks, was oozing slobbery goo. Dandy took it and pitched it to the back of the yard.

"So what now?" he asked again.

Malcolm mentally calculated the best approach. "Run!"

Malcolm and Dandy sped around the house to the gate. They nearly knocked it down pushing through. Malcolm closed it to keep the dogs in, but didn't bother with the lock.

Malcolm raced down the street like someone was chasing him. Dandy galloped beside him, keeping tempo with Malcolm's steps.

They nearly tripped over Cocoa in the front yard. She was stretched out in a chaise lounge, sunbathing.

"Watch it, slimeballs!" she yelled as she straightened her leopard print sunglasses with the butterscotch-yellow rhinestones.

They burst through the door, only to be met by Grandma Eunice. She was blocking their way with her wheelchair.

"Grandma, I need to get to the phone!"

"Have you seen him?" she asked, wearing a serious scowl.

"Seen who?"

"Bertram, that's who."

Malcolm fidgeted. "Grandma, no one's around right now. You don't have to pretend."

She looked Malcolm straight in the eye.

He could see her eyes were bright and clear. "I'm not pretending. I know he's around. I don't need that detector of yours to feel him. Have you seen him?"

Malcolm sighed. He knew he never should have filled in Grandma Eunice on his experience at the McBleaky House. Now she thought she could hunt ghosts, too. "No, I haven't. He's not here."

"Oh, he's here all right," she said. "I can sense him." She twirled her wheelchair around in a circle. "And I want my jellybeans!"

Malcolm and Dandy whipped around her and headed for the kitchen phone.

"9-1-1, what's your emergency?"

In the calmest voice possible, Malcolm said, "I'd like to report a break-in."

I'm Gonna Get You

Malcolm and Dandy sprinted out the door. They hurdled over Cocoa and hurried off. Minutes later, they plopped down on the lawn across the street from the Millers' house.

Then they waited. And waited . . . and waited . . . and waited. It was the second time that day that Malcolm had to wait on a government worker!

"How long has it been?" Dandy asked.

"Nearly ten minutes. They should be here soon."

Dandy ran his fingers through the clumps of clover where he sat. "Maybe they got lost."

"The police don't get lost," Malcolm informed him. "They have fancy GPS systems in their cars to guide them."

"Then maybe they're all busy with a bank robbery somewhere."

"Doubtful," Malcolm said.

"Or," Dandy continued, "maybe they thought we were just a couple of kids playing a prank, and they're not coming at all."

Dandy had a point. Malcolm hadn't thought of that. But the emergency dispatcher said he'd call it in. He hadn't acted like it was a prank.

Just when Malcolm was getting worried, he saw the police cruiser turning

the corner. The car rolled into the Millers' driveway, and Malcolm met the police officers who got out of the car.

"You the one who called in a break-in?" a squat, bald cop who resembled a bowling ball asked him.

"Yes, sir. The family is out of town," Malcolm told him.

The other cop leaned on the driver's side door. He was a lot younger and thinner, and his uniform looked like it was swallowing him whole.

"What are you boys doing poking around here if the family's gone?" the thin cop asked.

"I'm dogsitting for them while they're away," Malcolm quickly filled in the officers.

Dandy stood by him, twirling a clover between his fingers. His mouth was

hanging open, and Malcolm knew he was amazed that he was meeting real cops.

"Okay," the bowling ball cop said. "You boys wait back over there." He pointed across the street, where they had been waiting. "We'll check it out."

Malcolm didn't hesitate. He and Dandy hurried across the street. They stood, staring as the two policemen knocked on the front door.

When no one answered, the police peeked into windows. Malcolm and Dandy watched as they disappeared into the backyard. Brom and Bowser let out a few barks, but quickly stopped.

"This feels really dangerous," Dandy said, still twirling the clover.

"Yeah," Malcolm whispered. The entire street felt hushed and quiet except for the occasional call being reported on

the police car's radio. "We have a stalled car reported on Hansen Road."

Moments later the two cops emerged. The bowling ball cop looked toward them and shrugged. "Nothing in there."

Malcolm ran over. "But I saw him!"

"Maybe it was your imagination," the driver said. "You know, a trick of the light or something."

"Someone was in the house!" Malcolm argued. "I can show you where."

Both cops sighed as they followed Malcolm to the backyard. Dandy held the dogs while Malcolm led the cops to the kitchen window.

"He was in here," Malcolm told them.

The cops framed their faces with their hands and peered in.

"I don't see anything," the skinny cop said.

"Me neither," the bowling ball cop agreed.

Malcolm peeked in, too. Right there, next to the refrigerator, stood the same man he'd seen before.

"He's right there!" Malcolm shouted, trying to point through the glass.

The cops looked in again. When they didn't see anything, they glared at Malcolm.

"Are you playing games with us, kid?" the bowling ball cop sneered. "'Cause if you are, we might need to have a talk with your parents."

"But I see him! I swear I'm not making this up. I would never waste your time," Malcolm pleaded.

The skinny cop looked around and asked, "What is that annoying beeping?"

Malcolm looked down at the waistband of his jeans. His specter detector was suddenly going berserk.

The driver snorted. "Toys. Let's go, Jake," he said to the bowling ball cop. They trudged away.

Malcolm looked at Dandy. Dandy looked at Malcolm. They both looked down at the ghost detector. Then Malcolm dared another peek in through the kitchen window.

The figure had moved closer to the window now. Malcolm could make out every detail of his transparent face.

The man grinned at Malcolm and mouthed, "I'm gonna get you."

Breaking In

"Guess we don't have to go on a ghost hunt now, huh?" Dandy said, squirming around. Brom and Bowser were back, looking up at him with begging eyes.

"Yeah, but we only have the ghost detector with. I forgot to bring the ghost zapper," Malcolm complained.

"So now what?" Dandy asked, still wiggly.

"We come back after dinner," Malcolm said. "We can zap that ugly mullet then."

"We're not going in now?" Dandy asked with a relieved sigh.

"No," Malcolm answered. "We have to prepare."

"Good," Dandy said, wriggling like crazy. "'Cause I have to use the bathroom."

That evening Malcolm ripped into his fried chicken and mashed potatoes. He was eager to get a move on since this was his big chance to test the ghost zapper.

He was also eager to get away from the table. Cocoa had stayed outside too long and now had big white circles around her eyes where her sunglasses had been. She looked like a giant strawberry with a fungus.

"I'd rather have jellybeans!" Grandma Eunice complained through the entire meal. Malcolm shoveled his food down quickly to get away as fast as possible. The last thing he needed was for his mom to say he had to stay home with his grandma tonight.

He couldn't help but worry though. The ghost told him, "I'm gonna get you." Malcolm didn't take kindly to threats. Not even ghost threats. But he definitely had to proceed with caution.

The late afternoon sun hung low in the west. One thin cloud crossed it so it looked like a basketball sailing though the net. It was still a couple of hours till dark.

Malcolm waited for Dandy in the Millers' front yard. He had already turned the ghost detector to On so it'd be warmed up and ready.

Dandy approached commando style, ducking behind shrubs and the gate. He was wearing earmuffs and tinted safety goggles. He looked like a scientist CIA operative in the Arctic.

"What's all that for?" Malcolm asked.

"Huh?" Dandy said.

Malcolm removed the earmuffs. "What's with the extra gear?"

"The detector hypnotized me last time. I didn't want to take any chances."

Dandy made a good point. "I think it might be okay as long as you don't look at the blinking light too long," Malcolm explained.

"Oh," Dandy said, disappointed. "Can I keep the goggles on? They make everything look like I'm underwater." He did a mock breaststroke.

"Sure," Malcolm said. They headed around back.

Dandy stopped to pet the dogs. "Hey, Bowser. Hey, Brom."

Brom answered with a burpy-sounding bark.

"Shhhh!" Malcolm warned. "We want the element of surprise."

Dandy grinned. "I love surprises."

"Not a surprise for us, Dandy. We want to surprise the ghost . . . catch him off guard."

Dandy nodded, putting a finger to his lips. Then, the boys tiptoed toward the window.

Malcolm heard a yipping noise and looked toward the doghouse. There stood the small white dog. He was shaking.

Malcolm decided to check on the pooch once the Millers' ghost had been zapped. The poor thing looked frightened.

Malcolm peered into the window. Nothing was there. He scanned the entire kitchen.

"You see anything?" Dandy whispered.

"Not yet."

Malcolm's gaze moved to the open area that went from the kitchen to the living room. There, the ghost was lounging on the sofa, staring at the blank TV.

"Wait! I see him. Looks like he's watching ghost TV."

"Neat!" Dandy said. "I wonder what they show on that channel. . . . "

Malcolm motioned Dandy closer. "We have to find a way in."

They tried the window. Locked.

They tried the back door. Locked.

"We could slide down the chimney," Dandy suggested.

"That's too dangerous."

Dandy shrugged. "Maybe for you. But I'm wearing safety goggles, remember?"

"I've got a better idea," Malcolm told him. He stepped up onto the plastic container of dog food and ran his fingers along the top of the back door.

"Not there," he said. He jumped down and lifted the doormat. Nothing. Then he shoved the large dog food container aside. There it was—a shiny brass key.

Malcolm held it up in triumph. "See? This is better than sliding down the chimney."

Dandy shrugged. Malcolm could tell that Dandy was a tad disappointed. He knew Dandy had been ready to see how it felt to be Santa Claus.

As quietly as humanly possible, Malcolm slipped the key in and unlocked the door.

Come Out, Come Out, Wherever You Are

Click! Malcolm opened the door in slow-motion, careful of what might jump out. He looked left . . . then right. All clear.

He gently placed a foot inside. That's when Bowser and Brom decided to serenade them with some lonesome howls. It all felt too eerie to Malcolm.

Dandy crept in behind Malcolm and was about to shut the door. "Wait,"

Malcolm whispered. "Let's leave it open . . . just in case."

"In case of what?" Dandy whispered back, his goggles crooked on his face.

Malcolm wanted to say, "In case we have to make a run for it." But he didn't want to sound like a coward. "I think it's just safer that way," he said instead.

Dandy cocked his head to the side. "But what if the ghost gets out?"

"Then it probably won't haunt the Millers' house anymore and our job will be done."

Dandy looked thoughtful. "But I thought we're here to zap it, not chase it away." He made a vibrating motion like he was being zapped.

"We are," Malcolm argued. "But let's keep our options open, okay?"

"Okay," Dandy agreed. "We'll keep the door open . . . just like our options."

They tiptoed across the kitchen. Malcolm had his ghost detector at the ready. The amber light bleeped one pulse per second, meaning there was no ghost activity at the moment.

"Here's the plan," he whispered. "Once the ghost shows himself, I'll whip out the zapper and spray. Easy, right?"

"Shouldn't you keep it aimed?" Dandy wondered.

"I can draw it out fast," Malcolm said. He flipped his arm quickly to show Dandy his speed.

"But I thought you had to shake it first," Dandy reminded him.

"I'll shake it as I pull it out."

"You want me to hold it?" Dandy asked, adjusting his goggles.

"No! What if he recognizes what it is? It'll scare him off and we won't have a chance to zap him."

Dandy scrunched his face, confused. "Then he'll run out the kitchen door and our job will be done, right?"

"Just stay with me," Malcolm said, once again moving across the kitchen floor. Butterflies danced in his belly.

Bleep . . . bleep . . . bleep . . . bleep . . .

Malcolm moved cautiously, aiming the detector. He pointed it everywhere. At the oven. The refrigerator. The microwave.

"You think the ghost could be hiding in there?" Dandy asked.

Malcolm nodded. "Ghosts can fold themselves into anything."

"Really? 'Cause I saw a girl once at a magic show who could fold herself up and crawl into a cereal box."

"That was an illusion, Dandy. She didn't really fit into the cereal box."

"She could have," he said. "There wasn't any cereal in it."

Malcolm ignored him and kept his pace. The detector continued bleeping. He moved on, slinking through the kitchen.

He peered into the living room. The sun had dropped farther in the sky, and Malcolm had to squint to see into the darkened room. No ghost on the couch. The clock on the mantel kept time with the detector.

Malcolm aimed the specter detector at everything, including the portrait of the Millers. The family of four grinned "cheese!" out of the frame at him.

"Maybe we should turn on a light," Dandy said.

Malcolm shook his head. "It's not that dark."

"I can barely see a thing."

He heard Dandy stumble and saw him feeling around for objects in front of him. "Take off those goggles," Malcolm whispered.

"Oh, yeah." Dandy reluctantly pulled them down where they dangled around his neck.

Bleep, bleep, bleep, bleep, bleep, bleep!

The light on the ghost detector began to blink faster.

Suddenly, the TV clicked on. Malcolm jumped. Then he saw the remote lying on the coffee table, untouched. Yikes!

"Gee, I wonder what's on the ghost channel," Dandy said.

Only static and snow. Just as Malcolm reached for the remote, the picture cleared. A creepy phantom face looked out at them and grinned. "I'm gonna get you!"

Ghost Hunt

Malcolm clicked the off button on the TV several times. Dandy scrambled to put his goggles back on.

"Dude, what are you doing?" Malcolm yelled to him.

"I liked it better when I couldn't see!" Dandy said.

"Dandy!"

The phantom winked at Malcolm, and then the screen faded to black. Malcolm

shivered so hard he could barely hold the ghost detector steady.

Bleep . . . bleep . . . bleep . . . bleep . . .

"Why didn't you zap it?" Dandy asked.

"Because it wasn't really here. It was on TV. We've never used the ghost zapper, so we don't know what it will do. Who knows what would've happened if I'd zapped the screen."

"Yeah, and it is a flat-screen. That would've been expensive to replace," Dandy reasoned. "What'd we do now?"

Malcolm wondered that too. He glanced back at the TV. It now looked like a giant black hole, ready to swallow him up. He backed away quickly.

"Maybe we should look around some more."

"O-Okay," Dandy said, trying to sound brave.

Bleep . . . bleep . . . bleep . . . bleep . . .

The ghost detector was still at one bleep per second. Malcolm felt safe for the moment. "This way," he said.

He slowly inched his way to the hall, leading to the Millers' bedrooms. He'd barely taken two steps into it when he heard a loud crash! Malcolm flipped on the light and turned. Dandy lay sprawled out on the floor, face down. "Dandy!"

"Sorry," Dandy said, his voice muffled by the carpet. "I fell over the coffee table."

"Take off those goggles!"

Dandy did what Malcolm said, even though he felt safer with the goggles on. He caught up to Malcolm in the hallway.

Both boys stepped lightly. Malcolm held the detector with his left hand. He kept his right hand clutched around the

zapper. He wasn't taking chances. This nasty ghost could jump out at any moment, and Malcolm wanted to be able to whip out the zapper fast.

The boys crept up to the first bedroom. Malcolm peeked around the doorjamb. It was Katie Miller's room. She was the Millers' oldest daughter who went to high school. The walls were plastered with movie posters and silly street signs.

Bleep, bleep, bleep, bleep, bleep, bleep!

Dandy tapped Malcolm on the shoulder. "Does that guy look familiar to you?" He pointed to a poster of the old movie, *Gone with the Wind*. It showed the lead actor, Clark Gable, dipping the lead actress, Vivien Leigh. They were just about to kiss.

Malcolm took a step closer. *Gone with the Wind* was one of Grandma Eunice's

favorite movies. She made Malcolm watch it with her nearly every time he had to "watch" her for his parents. Malcolm could tell right away that this was not Clark Gable or any other character from the movie.

As though coming to life, the man's head turned and grinned at them. "I'm gonna get you!"

Malcolm pulled out the zapper and shook it hard. But as he aimed it, the face on the poster faded back to the original actor.

"Rats!" Malcolm yelled.

"I-I d-don't th-th-think we're going to g-get this one," Dandy said. His voice echoed like a stadium announcer's.

"I'm not giving up so easy," Malcolm announced.

This ghost was playing games with them. Like ghost hide-and-seek. There had to be a way to get him. Malcolm headed back into the hall.

Bleep . . . bleep . . . bleep . . . bleep . . .

"Come on," he told Dandy.

They did the usual tiptoe toward the next room.

"Who do you think it is?" Dandy asked.

"Who do I think who is?" Malcolm replied.

"The ghost. Who do you think he is and why do you think he's haunting the Millers' house?"

"I don't know," Malcolm said. "But he shouldn't be here."

"Maybe he should," Dandy argued. "Maybe he's guarding the house while the Millers are away."

"A guard ghost? I don't think so. He's not wearing a guard uniform or anything."

"Good point," Dandy said.

The next door led to the parents' bedroom. Malcolm flicked on the light and scanned the room. It was decorated with a blue striped bedspread, red striped curtains, and green striped wallpaper. The whole room looked like it was surrounded by bars.

Bleep, bleep, bleep, bleep, bleep, bleep!

Dandy headed toward a desk in the corner. "Look. They left their computer on. Let's Google something."

Malcolm pulled Dandy back fast. One of the fish bobbing along the screensaver turned and swam toward them.

"I'm gonna get you!" it gurgled. One of the bubbles floated off the screen and exploded near Dandy's face. He fell back on his bottom. The computer clicked off on its own.

"That's it!" Malcolm yelled. "I'm going to find you!" He pulled Dandy to his feet, and they stomped out of the room.

The next door he came to was shut. It was the bathroom. Malcolm only knew this because he could hear water running.

"Somebody's taking a shower," Dandy said.

Malcolm creaked the door open.

"I don't think we should go in," Dandy told him. "What if he's on the toilet?"

Malcolm ignored Dandy and opened the door. He motioned Dandy to follow him.

The shower curtain was drawn, and the room was covered in a hazy mist. "Look!" Dandy said, pointing to the mirror. Scrawled in the fogged up mirror were the words, *I'm gonna get you!*

Malcolm whipped around and pulled back the shower curtain. Nothing.

"One more room left to check," Malcolm said. But they never got the chance. As soon as the boys turned into hall, the ghost jumped down behind them and yelled, "Got you!"

Got You!

*B*leeeeeeeeeeeeeeeeeeeeeeeeeeeeeep!

Dandy screamed like a banshee while Malcolm shook the zapper. But before he pressed the trigger, the ghost huffed a horrendous breath at them. It knocked them down with hurricane force winds and sent the zapper flying out of Malcolm's hand.

"Ew!" Dandy said, waving his hand in front of his nose. "That smells like onions and feet!"

Malcolm couldn't argue. That ghost did have stinky breath. But he was more concerned with getting the zapper so he could finish this ghost off.

The ghost dived at them. The boys scrambled and ran. Malcolm saw the zapper had landed near the fireplace. He hurried toward it, but the ghost popped down, blocking his way. He reached his long bogeyman arms toward Malcolm.

"Do something!" Malcolm yelled.

Dandy grabbed his goggles by the strap and swung them at the ghost. "Take that!"

The ghost grabbed the goggles and pulled. Dandy pulled too. The strap stretched and stretched.

"Let go!" Malcolm cried.

Too late. The ghost let go first. The goggles snapped back, hitting Dandy in the head and knocking him flat . . . again.

"Ouch," he said groggily.

Malcolm needed to get that zapper! Or maybe he just needed to get away. The ghost tilted his head, looking at him this way and that. When he grinned again, he showed a full set of razor-like teeth. He started toward them.

Malcolm tried to get Dandy to his feet. The ghost moved closer . . . and closer . . . and . . . stopped.

The ghost's sneer turned to surprise. Malcolm heard snarling and looked down. The little white dog had come in through the open kitchen door and was biting the ghost's leg. He was even dragging him backward.

The ghost tried shaking him off. He jumped and kicked and twisted his leg. The fierce little dog held on tight. The distraction was exactly what Malcolm

needed. He grabbed the ghost zapper and shook.

When the ghost turned back it was Malcolm's turn to grin and yell, "I'm gonna get you!"

The little dog let go as Malcolm pulled the trigger. The zapper sprayed the specter with a thick spatter of purple ooze. The ooze looked a lot like whipped cream, but it smelled like cotton candy.

The ghost stood frozen in goo. Then he and the goo slowly melted into nothing more than a large wet stain on the carpet.

The little dog sniffed it. *Yip! Yip!*

"Yes!" Malcolm cheered.

Dandy sat up, rubbing his forehead. "Is it over?"

"Yeah," Malcolm answered. "Thanks to this little fellow—" But when he turned back, the little dog had already run off.

Dandy looked at the large wet spot on the carpet. "Did the dog do that?"

Malcolm smiled. "Not exactly. Come on, let's go." He pointed to the big purple lump now forming just above Dandy's eyes. "You need to put some ice on that."

Malcolm helped his friend up and they hurried out. Then, he locked the back door and put the key back in its place under the plastic container. Brom and Bowser had joined them on the porch. Bowser held the rubber ball in his jowls.

"Not now," Malcolm said. He looked out at the doghouse. Was the brave little white dog curled up in the corner? He didn't have time to check. It was dark now, and he needed to get home.

When they reached the front yard, Malcolm turned to Dandy. "Thanks," he said.

Dandy looked puzzled. "For what?"

"For helping me out. I would've been too scared to do this alone."

"Yeah, me too. It's too bad we'll never know who that ghost was," Dandy said.

They left the Millers' house, ghost-free, and headed home.

Spooky

Malcolm walked Dandy to his house and made sure he put an ice pack on his forehead. It was late by the time he got home.

He was met with a surprise as he reached his front porch.

Bleep, bleep, bleep, bleep, bleep, bleep!

The specter detector was going off like crazy. Malcolm had forgotten to turn it off. As he reached to get it out of his pocket, he had a second surprise.

Yip! Yip! Yip!

The little dog from the Millers' house sat on his porch, excitedly wagging his tail.

"Hey, fella," Malcolm said, bending down. "How'd you find my house?"

The dog answered with *Yip!*

The dog didn't have a collar like Bowser and Brom. And Malcolm hadn't seen an extra bowl or bed back at the Millers'. There was really no sign that the dog belonged to them.

The mutt sat, looking up at Malcolm with large pleading eyes. Malcolm had never owned a dog, thanks to Cocoa and her sneezing fits. But maybe he could sneak this one in and keep it in his lab. At least for a while.

"Okay, you win," Malcolm said. He reached down to pick up the dog. To his

amazement, his hand passed right through it.

Malcolm jumped back. "Whoa! That's spooky."

Yip! Yip! The ghostly dog excitedly wagged his tail.

"Spooky," Malcolm repeated. "Come on, Spooky. Come on, boy." He opened his front door, and his new dog, Spooky, ran in.

The house was dark and quiet. Exhausted, Malcolm decided to go straight to bed. There'd been way too much excitement tonight.

As they trudged through the kitchen, Spooky began to bark and the ghost detector started bleeping up a storm. Malcolm looked around. To his amazement, a transparent man stood in the doorway!

Startled, Malcolm jumped. The man was wearing a powder-blue '70s leisure suit and was smiling at him. Malcolm thought about grabbing his ghost zapper, but this apparition didn't appear menacing at all. In fact, he looked kind and proud. Malcolm then saw a bit of family resemblance.

"Grandpa Bertram, is that you?"

Grandpa Bertram nodded. Without a word, he pointed to the kitchen table, then disappeared.

Malcolm looked down to see a small bag filled with jellybeans. He picked them up, careful not to mess up the lovely blue ribbon attached. He quietly crept to Grandma Eunice's room and placed them on her night table.

Then Malcolm happily went off to bed. When he turned off the specter detector,

Spooky disappeared. He quickly turned it back on and could see his new pooch. He smiled, knowing for certain that Cocoa wouldn't be having sneezing fits with this pet!

Malcolm said good night to Spooky, shut off his ghost detector, and fell into a dead sleep.

FIVE MORE WAYS TO DETECT A GHOST, SPIRIT, OR POLTERGEIST

From Ghost Detectors Malcolm and Dandy

6. Ghosts often hide out in empty houses. If you are watching a neighbor's house, check the windows before getting too close.

7. Seeing transparent people in dark windows is a definite sign of ghosts.

8. Remember that dogs are more sensitive to ghosts than people. Watch your dog to see if it barks at thin air.

9. Ghosts can also give off a disgusting smell. Is there a smell of rotting onions mixed with feet nearby?

10. Not all ghosts are mean. If you find stray bags of jellybeans lying around, they may be a gift from a relative. Just in case though, turn on your specter detector and wait for the bleep!